Little T and Lizard the Wizard

written and illustrated by
Frank Rodgers

PICTURE WINDOW BOOKS
Minneapolis, Minnesota

Editor: Nick Healy
Page Production: Brandie E. Shoemaker
Creative Director: Keith Griffin
Editorial Director: Carol Jones

First American edition published in 2007 by
Picture Window Books
5115 Excelsior Boulevard
Suite 232
Minneapolis, MN 55416
877-845-8392
www.picturewindowbooks.com

First published in 2002 by A&C Black Publishers Limited, 38 Soho Square, London W1D 3HB, with the title LIZARD THE WIZARD.

Printed in the United States of America.

Library of Congress Cataloging-in-Publication Data
Rodgers, Frank, 1944-
Little T and Lizard the Wizard / by Frank Rodgers. — 1st American ed.
p. cm. — (Read-it! chapter books)
Summary: Upon learning that the Royal Magician is nervous about his upcoming Moment of Magic, Little T decides to help out but soon the entire kingdom learns that the young prince is not yet ready to be a wizard.
ISBN-13: 978-1-4048-2725-7 (hardcover)
ISBN-10: 1-4048-2725-0 (hardcover)
[1. Wizards—Fiction. 2. Magic—Fiction. 3. Self-confidence—Fiction. 4. Tyrannosaurus rex—Fiction. 5. Dinosaurs—Fiction.] I. Title. II. Series.
PZ7.R6154Litb 2006
[E]—dc22 2006003418

Table of Contents

Magic
Made

Chapter One

Little Prince T Rex strolled through the castle. It was a sunny morning, and all around him he could hear dinosaurs being happy.

His royal dad, King High T the Mighty, sang in the bathtub.

His royal mom, Queen Teena Regina, played her trumpet for Little T's royal sister.

The royal cook whistled merrily as he baked the sweet rolls.

The royal guards tap-danced up and down instead of marching.

Everyone is cheery this morning.

Chapter Two

But as he turned a corner, Little T bumped into the royal magician, Lizard the Wizard.

Lizard the Wizard looked very gloomy. "What's wrong?" asked Little T.

Everyone is happy except you!

The royal magician groaned. "No wonder," he replied. "Every year I have to perform a special piece of magic to entertain the dinosaurs."

It's called the Magic Moment.
Cool!

"Rotten, you mean," sighed Lizard the Wizard. "You see, I'm not very good at Magic Moments. I get very nervous, and they all become disasters."

Last year, I tried to make lovely new clothes appear on all of the dinosaurs.
And did you?

"Fat chance," replied Lizard the Wizard glumly. "I put on my best hat, used my new wand, and tried my strongest spell."

Guess what happened.
What?

"Instead of creating new clothes, I just made their old clothes disappear!

ZAP!

"There they were, standing around in their underwear," said Lizard the Wizard. "They weren't pleased."

They won't be looking forward to this year's Magic Moment.

Little T thought for a moment. “I know,” he said brightly. “Why don’t you let me help you?”

I’m sure I’d be great at doing magic.
I’ve always wanted to be a wizard like you.

The royal magician looked doubtful. “I don’t know,” he said slowly.

It might not be such a good idea.

Little T followed Lizard the Wizard to his room.

It was full of books and bottles, cauldrons and candles, and potions and powders.

"Cool," said Little T, looking around. "I really would like to be a wizard."

Let me try. Please?

"I don't know," sighed Lizard the Wizard again.

Magic is nothing to fool with, you know.

"But I'm sure I can do it," said Little T confidently. He snatched a book from a dusty shelf. It was called *Magic Made Easy*.

I'll use this!

"Hold on a minute," protested the royal magician.

"Don't worry," said Little T. "It'll be all right. I'll just read the book."

Then I can help you with the Magic Moment.
But ...

Little T dashed off.

Everyone will be surprised!

Chapter Three

Everyone was surprised. Little T didn't just read the magic book. He tried out some of the spells.

The first ones to be surprised were his good friends Don, Bron, Tops, and Dinah.

They were doing their homework.

"This homework will take ages to do," groaned Bron.

"Forever," said Tops.

"Don't worry," said Little T.

This will be the fastest study session ever!

He read a spell out loud.

ZOOM!

Their notebooks soared off.

“Oops!” gasped Little T as his friends ran after their notebooks.

I didn’t expect the homework to go that fast!
Magic Made easy

The second ones to be surprised were the royal builders. They were busy repairing a wall.

"Phew!" said one. "This basket of bricks is heavy."

"Don't worry," said Little T.

I'll make it lighter!

He read out a magic spell.

FLASH!

"Help!" the royal builders cried as the basket whisked them up to the ceiling like a hot-air balloon.

Oops! I didn't mean to make it so light!

The royal builders managed to climb down their ladders.

Then they covered the basket and nailed it to the floor until the spell wore off.

The next ones to be surprised were Little T's mom and dad. They were having breakfast. King High T the Mighty held up his sausages. "These are a bit small," he complained.

Two bites and they're gone!
Royal Jam

"Nothing I can do about it, dear," said Queen Teena.

"Don't worry, Dad!" called Little T.

I can make them bigger!

He read a spell out loud.

WHOOOSH!

The sausages grew as big as pillows and knocked High T off his chair.

"Little T!" cried his mom. "Take that book of spells back to the royal magician."

At once!

"And don't mess with any more magic," sputtered his dad from underneath a giant sausage.

It'll take me all week to eat this thing!

Chapter Four

Little T couldn't resist one more try. As he passed a window, he looked down into the courtyard.

The dinosaurs were there, waiting for the royal magician to perform this year's Magic Moment.

They all looked anxious.

It'll be as bad as last year.
It will be twice as bad!
I'm really worried.
I'm twice as worried.

Little T had an idea. “Don’t worry,” he said.

I’ll use magic to make your worries shrink.
You’ll be surprised!

The dinosaurs were quite surprised. Little T's magic didn't make their worries shrink.

FLASH!

It made the dinosaurs shrink!

"What's going on?" they cried. "We're the size of mice!"

The dinosaurs' dogs and cats thought the dinosaurs really were mice and chased after them. Dinosaurs darted this way and that, trying not to get gobbled up by their own pets!

"Help!" cried the dinosaurs, scurrying around in panic.

Little T dashed outside. His friends were returning with their notebooks. "Thank goodness!" he gasped.

Quick! Help me save the dinosaurs!

Don, Bron, Tops, and Dinah dashed all over the courtyard with Little T.

They managed to pick up all of the tiny dinosaurs and put them in a cardboard box. "It's all your fault!" the dinosaurs squeaked at Little T.

Change us back to normal!

Little T blushed. “I don’t know how to,” he said.

Only Lizard the Wizard can do that.

“Then go and get him!” cried the tiny dinosaurs.

Hurry!

Chapter Five

Little T left Don to look after the box full of dinosaurs.

Little T, Bron, Tops, and Dinah rushed off to look for the royal magician. But Lizard the Wizard was nowhere to be found.

He had decided to hide, so he wouldn't disgrace himself again at the Magic Moment.

"Where can he be?" cried Little T. He and his friends looked everywhere.

They checked under royal beds,

behind royal curtains, and inside royal cupboards.

Royal
Stuff

But Lizard the Wizard seemed to have disappeared. Disappointed, the friends went back to the courtyard.

"I wonder if he used a vanishing spell?" murmured Little T.

It's possible.

Then he heard a muffled sneeze come from behind him. He turned around, but there was nothing there except a suit of armor.

Aha!

Climbing on his friends' shoulders, Little T reached up and lifted the visor of the helmet.

Achoo! Lizard the Wizard sneezed.

It's dusty in here.

“You have to come out,” said Little T.

The dinosaurs need you.
No, they don't.
Yes, they do!

Quickly, he told the royal magician what had happened.

Lizard the Wizard looked nervous. "Oh dear," he said. "I suppose I will have to help them, won't I?"

He climbed out of the suit of armor and followed Little T and his friends across the courtyard.

The royal magician gasped when he saw what was in the cardboard box. "Nice bit of magic," he whispered to Little T. "I'm impressed."

It's better than I could do.

Little T shook his head. "It was an accident," he whispered back.

The tiny dinosaurs waved at Lizard the Wizard. "Thank goodness you're here!" they squeaked.

Thank you for coming!

Lizard the Wizard smiled. It was the first time the dinosaurs had ever been pleased to see him.

Suddenly, he didn't feel nervous anymore. He knew he could not let them down. He needed a perfect Magic Moment, with no mistakes. He concentrated hard. Shutting his eyes and crossing his fingers, he chanted a powerful spell.

FLASH!

The courtyard filled with normal-sized dinosaurs again. "You did it!" they cried in delight. "A perfect Magic Moment!"

Hooray for Lizard the Wizard!

Lizard the Wizard smiled. At last, one of his pieces of magic had worked. But he knew it might not go as well the next time. He held up his hands. "Dinosaurs!" he said.

I have come to a decision.

"That was the last Magic Moment I will ever perform. It was terrific, I agree," he said.

Always leave them wanting more. That's my motto!

Being polite, the dinosaurs pretended they were disappointed. "Oh, it can't be," they said.

You can't stop now.
Really, you can't.

Little T thought they meant it.

"Don't worry!" he cried. "I've always wanted to be a wizard. You will have a Magic Moment next year!"

I'll do it!

Don, Bron, Tops, and Dinah gasped. "No, you won't!" they cried. "No more magic!" They snatched away the book of spells.

We're going to hide this!

"That's no problem," said Little T. "I think I remember some of the spells."

I don't need the book.

He grinned and said, "Next year's Magic Moment will be the best!"

Everyone groaned, but Little T laughed. "You just wait," he said.

You'll be surprised!

Magic Made easy

Look for More *Read-it!* Chapter Books

Grandpa's Boneshaker Bicycle	978-1-4048-2732-5
Jenny the Joker	978-1-4048-2733-2
Little T and the Crown Jewels	978-1-4048-2726-4
Little T and the Dragon's Tooth	978-1-4048-2727-1
Little T and the Royal Roar	978-1-4048-2728-8
The Minestrone Mob	978-1-4048-2723-3
Mr. Croc Forgot	978-1-4048-2731-8
Mr. Croc's Silly Sock	978-1-4048-2730-1
Mr. Croc's Walk	978-1-4048-2729-5
The Peanut Prankster	978-1-4048-2724-0
Silly Sausage and the Little Visitor	978-1-4048-2735-6
Silly Sausage and the Spooks	978-1-4048-2736-3
Silly Sausage Goes to School	978-1-4048-2738-7
Silly Sausage in Trouble	978-1-4048-2737-0
Stan the Dog and the Crafty Cats	978-1-4048-2739-4
Stan the Dog and the Golden Goals	978-1-4048-2740-0
Stan the Dog and the Major Makeover	978-1-4048-2741-7
Stan the Dog and the Sneaky Snacks	978-1-4048-2742-4
Uncle Pat and Auntie Pat	978-1-4048-2734-9

Looking for a specific title? A complete list of *Read-it!* Chapter Books is available on our Web site:
www.picturewindowbooks.com